James Howe

illustrated by Marie-Louise Gay

CANDLEWICK PRESS

Contents

Houndsley and Catina
1

Houndsley and Catina
and the Birthday Surprise
41

Houndsley and Catina
and the Quiet Time
87

Houndsley and Catina
Plink and Plunk
133

Houndsley
and
Catina

for Amelia Englund Keller

J. H.

Contents

Chapter One: The Writer 5

Chapter Two: Cooking Contest . . . 15

Chapter Three: fireflies 33

Chapter One
The Writer

Catina wanted to be a writer.

Every evening after dinner, she would make herself a cup of ginger tea and sit down to write another chapter in her book.

So far she had written seventy-three chapters.

The book was called *Life Through the Eyes of a Cat.*

"My book will win prizes," Catina told her best friend, Houndsley, one day when he asked how the writing was going.

"I did not ask if your book was going to win prizes," Houndsley said in his soft-as-a-rose-petal voice. "I asked how the writing was going."

"I will be famous," Catina went on as if she had not heard him.

Houndsley sighed. “May I read your book?” he asked.

“Of course,” said Catina. “I have only one chapter left to write.”

The next evening, Catina invited Houndsley to her house.

"Here is my book," she said proudly. She gave him all seventy-four chapters, a cup of ginger tea, and a plate of cookies.

"I will need more cookies," said Houndsley.

Catina did not take her eyes off Houndsley while he read. He wished the phone would ring so she would have to go to another room.

Here is some of what Houndsley read:

On the subject of mice,
enough cannot ~~bee~~ be said.
But who am I to say?
I have known many mice
in my life. They are all
right. For rodents.
Well, I am bored
writing ~~abut~~ about mice.
Who cares, anyway?

Oh, dear, Houndsley thought. *Catina is a terrible writer. What am I going to say to her?*

"I am at a loss for words," Houndsley told Catina when he had finished reading the book. "I am speechless."

Catina beamed. "My writing has left you speechless?" she exclaimed. "Now I know I will be a famous writer! Oh, thank you, Houndsley!"

"You're welcome," Houndsley said.

But he was thinking, *Oh, dear. Poor Catina.*

Chapter Two
Cooking Contest

Every Saturday night, Houndsley cooked dinner for his best friend, Catina, and his next-door neighbor Bert.

This was not always easy. Even though she was a cat, Catina did not eat meat. And what Bert liked best were seeds, grains, and worms.

But Houndsley did not mind. He enjoyed cooking. And he was good at it.

One Saturday night, Bert said, "Everything you make is delicious, Houndsley. I've never had worms with poppy seeds and broccoli before."

“Worms?!” Catina yelped. “You know I’m a vegetarian!”

“They are not real worms,” Houndsley assured his friend. “They only look like worms. They are made of tofu.”

Catina laughed. "You are a wonder," she said.

"Yes," said Bert. "You should enter the cooking contest."

"Cooking contest? Oh, I don't know about that," Houndsley said, his voice growing softer with each word.

"But you are a great cook!" Catina cried. "You could be famous!"

"Do you think so?" Houndsley asked.

"I know so!" said Catina. "When you have a talent as big as yours, you must share it with the world!"

"Really?"

“First prize is a set of pots and pans,” said Bert.

“I could use a new set of pots and pans,” said Houndsley, although he already had so many he was not sure where he would put them. “All right, I will do it!”

On the day of the cooking contest, Houndsley arrived with everything he needed.

"I am going to make my three-bean chili," Houndsley told Catina and Bert, who had come to cheer him on.

"Your three-bean chili is delicious," Catina told him. "You will win."

Houndsley blushed. He thought he might win, too, but he did not dare to say so.

“I did not know so many others would be here,” Houndsley said.

“Look, Houndsley,” said Bert. “You are going to be on television!”

Oh, dear, Houndsley thought. *Everyone will be watching me.*

Rice

Houndsley had made his three-bean chili many times before, but today everything went wrong.

He dropped a can of tomatoes on his foot.

He did not cook the rice long enough.

And he forgot to put in the beans.

All three kinds!

When the judges came to taste his chili, they made faces.

"I think I broke a tooth on the rice," one of them said.

"I don't taste the beans," said another.

“Maybe you should call this no-bean chili,” said a third, and all the judges laughed.

Houndsley had never been so embarrassed in his life.

"I will never cook again," he told Catina and Bert.

"Not even for us?" Bert said.

"Maybe for you," said Houndsley. "But please do not ask for three-bean chili."

Chapter Three
Fireflies

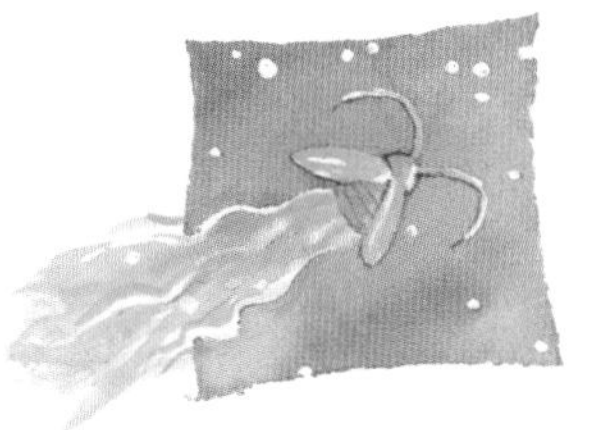

One night, Houndsley and Catina were sitting outside watching fireflies. This was one of their favorite things to do together.

They sat quietly for a long time.

At last, Houndsley said, "I did not need a new set of pots and pans. I only wanted to win that contest to show everyone I was the best cook."

"You are the best cook," Catina said.

"I do not need to be the best," said Houndsley in his soft-as-a-rose-petal voice. "I just enjoy cooking. Trying to be the best made me nervous, and I did not have fun. If you do not have fun doing something you like to do, what is the point?"

Catina thought about this.

“I do not have fun writing,” she said as they began to walk. “My mind wanders and I get bored.”

A firefly blinked at her.

“I want to be a famous writer,” she went on, “but I do not like to write.”

“Perhaps you will be famous at something else,” said Houndsley.

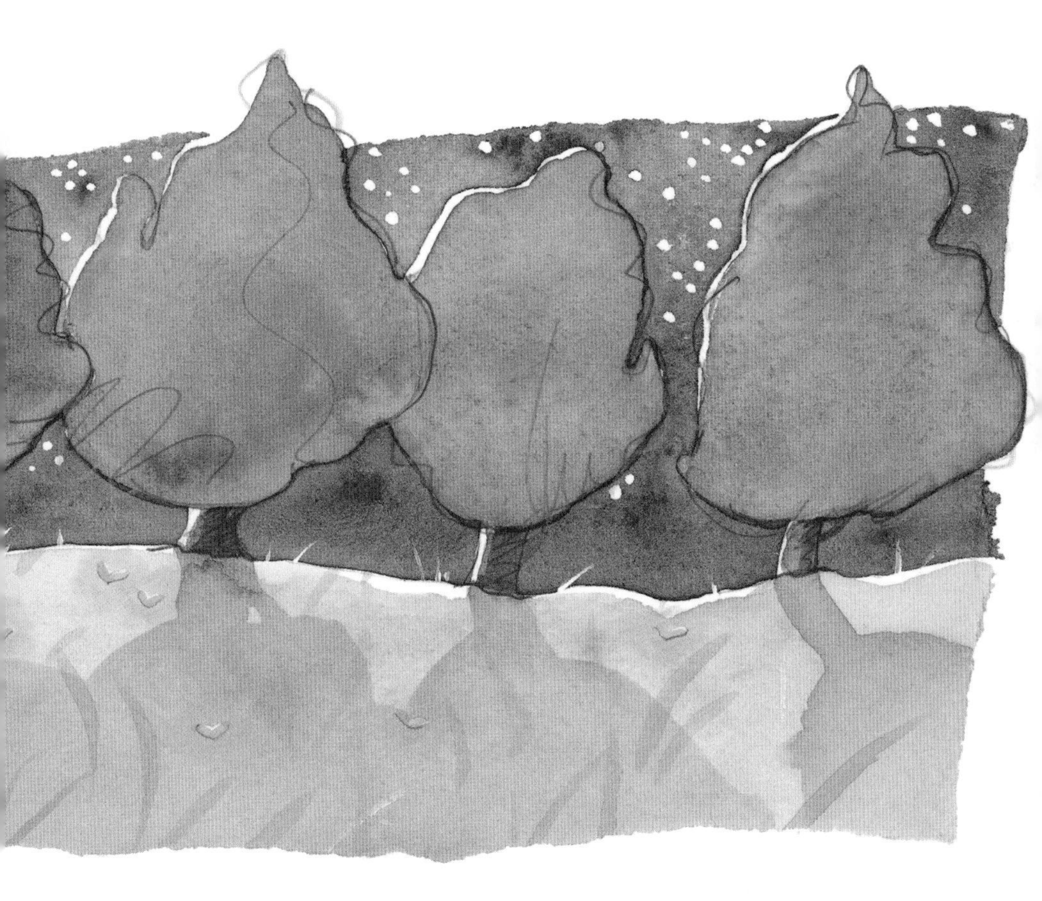

"Yes," Catina said. "First I will find something I like to do. Then I will do it and do it and do it until I am very good at it. And then I might be famous."

"I know something you are good at already," said Houndsley, "although you will never be famous for it."

"What?"

"Being my friend."

Catina began to purr. "Being your friend is better than being famous," she said.

Houndsley and Catina came to their favorite spot. They sat for a long time. They did not talk about winning prizes or being famous. They did not talk about anything. They smelled the sweet summer air and listened to crickets. They watched the fireflies dance and blink and light up the night in front of them.

Everyone has talents. Watching fireflies was one of theirs.

and the Birthday Surprise

for Esme Elizabeth and Phoebe Genevieve

J. H.

Contents

Chapter One: Sad .45

Chapter Two: The Cake 55

Chapter Three: The Surprise 67

Chapter One
Sad

Houndsley was sad.

"Are you sad because it is raining?"

Catina asked.

Houndsley shook his head.

"I like the rain," he told her.

Catina thought. "Are you sad because there are holes in your sweater?" she asked.

Houndsley shook his head again.

"This sweater is very old," he said. "And moths have to eat, too. I do not feel sad because there are holes in my sweater."

“Well then, are you sad because you wish you were doing something else?”

Houndsley looked surprised.

“I am never sad because I wish I were doing something else,” he told Catina. “If I wanted to be doing something else, I would go and do it.”

"Then why are you sad?" asked Catina.

"I am sad because I do not know when my birthday is," Houndsley told his friend.

"Oh," said Catina.

She wanted to say something to cheer Houndsley up.

But all she could think to say was, “I do not know when my birthday is either.”

The two friends walked quietly in the rain until they came to Houndsley's house.

"Do you want to come in?" Houndsley asked.

Catina shook her head. "I should go home," she said.

As he watched her walk away, Houndsley thought, *Oh, dear. Now Catina is sad, too.*

Chapter Two
The Cake

For the next two days, Houndsley did not see much of Catina. She did not jog by his house each morning, calling out hello. She did not invite him to join her each evening for yoga and ginger tea. He missed her and worried that something was wrong.

When he bumped into her in town and asked how she was feeling, Catina said, “Oh, I’m fine,” and hurried away.

Catina does not seem fine, Houndsley thought. *I think she is still sad.*

Suddenly, he had an idea.

"I will bake a cake for Catina," he told himself. "A cake will make her feel better."

Houndsley made a list of everything he would need. He even thought to include rainbow sprinkles, which he did not like but he knew Catina loved. Off he went to the market. He could not wait to start baking!

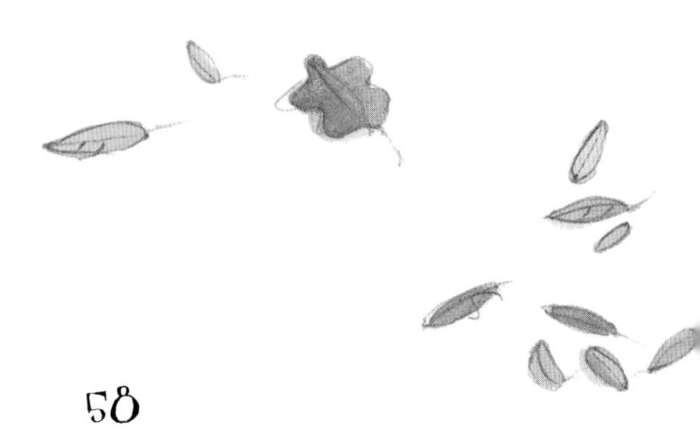

Houndsley was very good at baking, but he always made a mess. It was not long before he was covered in flour and sugar and chocolate.

When his next-door neighbor Bert dropped in, Houndsley explained what he was doing.

"Is it Catina's birthday?" Bert asked.

"No," said Houndsley. "At least, I do not think so. I do not know when Catina's birthday is."

This gave Houndsley another idea. "Bert, will you help me?"

"Of course," said Bert. "By the way, that cake smells yummy. I don't suppose you put any worms in it, did you?"

"I am sorry," Houndsley said. "If I were baking this cake for you, I would have put in worms. But this cake is for Catina, and Catina does not like worms."

Bert shook out his feathers. "We all have our own tastes," he said. "Now, how can I help you?"

"While I finish the cake, will you ask our friends to come to my house tonight at seven o'clock?"

"Are you having a party?" Bert asked.

"Yes," said Houndsley. "A surprise birthday party for Catina. Even though today may not be her birthday."

Bert thought for a moment. "I guess I should not ask Catina to come to your house."

"No," Houndsley said. "I will call Catina later. I will tell her I am still feeling sad and I need her to come over and cheer me up."

"You are very clever," said Bert.

"Thank you," said Houndsley, feeling pleased with himself.

"Well, I'm off," said Bert.

Chapter Three
The Surprise

It took Houndsley the rest of the afternoon to finish the cake.

"Catina will be so happy," Houndsley said. "I have never made anything so beautiful, and I have made it just for her."

He looked around at his messy kitchen and at the clock on the shelf.

"I will just have time to get everything cleaned up before the guests arrive," he said. "But first I should call Catina."

Just then, the phone rang.

"Hello, Houndsley. This is Catina. I am sorry to bother you, but there is a crack in my bathtub. Could you help me fix it?"

Oh, dear, Houndsley thought. *I cannot say no to a friend who is asking for help.*

"I'll be right there," said Houndsley.

"Thank you," said Catina.

Houndsley thought, *If I can fix the crack in the bathtub really quickly, I will still be able to get Catina to my house by seven o'clock. I will just have to think of an excuse to get her here.*

Houndsley hurried to clean up the mess he had made.

A few minutes before six-thirty, he rang the doorbell of Catina's house.

"I will have to fix that crack quickly," Houndsley told Catina when she opened the door.

But before he could say another word, he heard "SURPRISE!"

There were all his friends, crowded into Catina's little living room.

HOUNDSLEY

Houndsley was confused.

"What about the crack in the bathtub?" he asked.

"There is no crack in the bathtub," said Catina. "I just made that up to get you here."

Then she handed Houndsley a present.

"What is it?" he asked.

"Open it and find out," said Catina.

Houndsley opened the box and pulled out a sweater. A sweater as soft as Houndsley's rose-petal voice. A sweater with no holes made by hungry moths.

"I knitted it for you myself," Catina told Houndsley. "I have not had time to do anything else for the past two days. Happy birthday! Even though today may not be your birthday."

"I have never seen such a beautiful sweater," Houndsley said, slipping it on. It fit perfectly.

Suddenly, Bert rushed in from the kitchen.

“Catina! Houndsley! Something is burning!” he squawked.

Houndsley and Catina ran into the kitchen. They looked in the oven, but nothing was burning. They sniffed the air. Nothing was burning!

"What's the matter with Bert?" Catina asked.

“And where did everyone go?” Houndsley said when they went back into an empty living room.

There was a note on the table:

Houndsley,
you left something
at your house.
Go home and get it.
And bring Catina
with you.
Your friend,
Bert

"Bert is acting very strangely," said Catina. "I think he has been eating too many worms."

But Houndsley guessed what Bert was up to. If he was right, he knew where everyone had gone.

SURPRISE!

all their friends shouted when

Houndsley opened the door

to his house.

"I have never seen such a beautiful cake!" Catina exclaimed.

"I baked it for you myself," Houndsley said proudly.

"I have never been invited to two surprise birthday parties on the same day!" said their friend Moxie.

"We did not know we had the same birthday before this," said Houndsley.

"But we do now," Catina said.

Houndsley showed everyone his new sweater.

Catina blew out the candles on her cake.

And the two friends decided right then and there that every year after that, they would celebrate their birthdays together on the very same day.

and the Quiet Time

To Mark,
and our quiet times together
J. H.

Contents

Chapter One: Silent White 91

Chapter Two: The Island 103

Chapter Three: The Concert 119

Chapter One
Silent White

It was the first snow of the winter.

Houndsley gazed out his window at the silent white falling everywhere. The world had no shadows, only white on white on white.

"It is the quiet time," Houndsley said in his soft-as-a-rose-petal voice.

Catina listened.

"It is too quiet," she said.

"Oh," said Houndsley. "But that is why this is my favorite time of year. In the quiet time, everything stops. I think we may be snowed in."

"Snowed in?" Catina cried, jumping up to join Houndsley at the window. "But this is terrible. What about the concert tonight? I was going to get my whiskers curled and buy a new dress. And we're in charge of refreshments."

"We have all day to bake cookies," Houndsley said. "Your whiskers look fine just the way they are, and you have plenty of dresses you can wear. The stores might not even be open today. It's a storm, Catina. There's nothing to do but enjoy it. Isn't it beautiful?"

“A storm isn’t beautiful,” Catina replied. “A storm means not being able to do all the things we had planned on doing. Oh, no!”

“What is it?” Houndsley asked.

“What if we can’t have our concert? We have been practicing for months!”

“What will be, will be,” Houndsley told his friend. “Let’s enjoy the day. We can still practice, and if there is a concert tonight, we will be ready for it!”

Houndsley returned to his cello.

Catina picked up her clarinet.

Before they began to play, Houndsley said, "Listen, Catina. Can you hear it?"

“Hear what?”

“The quiet. It is almost like music.”

Suddenly, there was a loud crash from the house next door. Houndsley's neighbor Bert was practicing for his part in the concert. Bert played the cymbals.

"Houndsley," said Catina, "I do not think Bert understands about the quiet time."

Chapter Two
The Island

The snow kept falling.

All morning, Catina fretted about her plans for the day.

All morning, Houndsley told her not to fret.

Finally, Houndsley said, "Let's pretend that we are on an island. We can't go anywhere. Let's see, what do we have on the island with us?"

"I don't suppose we have a whisker curler, do we?" asked Catina.

"No, but we do have books," said Houndsley. He pulled a book from the shelf and sat down on the sofa, patting the cushion next to him. "Let's read poems to each other. I'll start."

At first, Catina had a hard time paying attention. She looked out the window and wished that the snow would stop. But when it was her turn to read, she found a poem that made her laugh.

And then Houndsley read a poem that made her cry.

“I am not a very good writer,” she told Houndsley after they had read for a while longer, “but it might be fun to write poems. Even bad ones.”

“I think there may be paper and pencils on this island,” said Houndsley.

For a long time, the two friends wrote poems and read them to each other.

"I'm sleepy," said Catina. "My brain is tired."

"Why don't you take a nap while I fix lunch?" Houndsley suggested.

"Good idea," said Catina with a yawn.

* * *

After lunch, Houndsley and Catina baked cookies.

Then they played board games, because there were board games on their island, too.

There were also logs on their island. Houndsley and Catina built a fire and talked about what they saw in the flames. And then they grew still and didn't talk at all.

At last, Catina said, "I think there are dreams on this island."

"What do you mean?" Houndsley asked.

"Oh, I was just dreaming about all the things I would like to do someday. And then I thought that dreaming about them is almost as good as doing them."

Houndsley nodded. "Sometimes dreaming is even better than making plans," he said.

Soon it was late afternoon. The house was growing cold.

"We need more logs," said Houndsley. "I will climb out a window to get some. I can't open my doors because of all the snow."

"I will go with you," Catina said.

Houndsley and Catina almost forgot about getting the logs. They were too busy building snow creatures and making snow angels and catching snowflakes on their tongues.

A sudden *crash* sent them scrambling to get their logs and climb back inside.

As Houndsley rebuilt the fire, Catina returned from the kitchen with a pot of ginger tea.

Another *crash* was heard.

"On the island next door," Catina said, "there are cymbals."

Chapter Three
The Concert

The sound of cymbals crashing was replaced by the sound of a shovel scraping against the sidewalk in front of Houndsley's house.

"Houndsley! Catina!" cried Bert. "It's time to go to the concert!"

Houndsley and Catina looked out to see their friends and neighbors trudging through the snow with their instruments.

"But I have to go to my house and change my clothes," said Catina.

"No one will see a fancy dress under a coat," said Houndsley. "Besides, a concert is for listening, not for looking."

Houndsley handed Catina her coat and a pair of snowshoes.

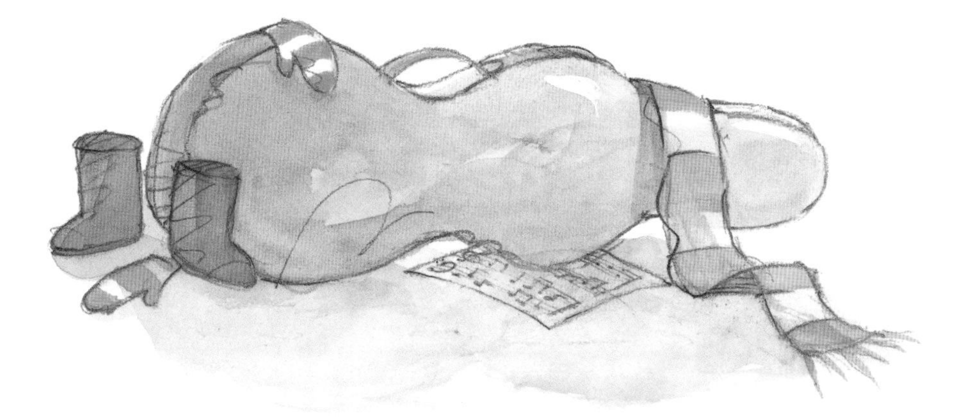

"I have been practicing all day," Bert said excitedly to his friends as they slowly made their way through the snow.

Houndsley and Catina smiled at each other and said nothing.

"I am sad that we have left our island," Catina whispered to Houndsley as they joined the others at the light-strung gazebo in the park. "I like the quiet time."

Houndsley nodded. "I was looking forward to this concert," he said, "but it seems a shame to make noise tonight. Even if the noise is music."

As the musicians took their places in the gazebo, a small audience gathered. The houses around the park had their windows open so that those inside could listen, too.

Without saying a word, the musicians picked up their instruments and began to play so softly that the notes fell on the listening ears like snowflakes on waiting tongues, gently, softly, there for a flicker before melting away.

Houndsley began to worry that Bert would ruin everything. Bert's only part was to play the final note of the final piece of music. *How awful,* Houndsley thought, *to end the evening with a crash.*

But when the last note came, it was not a crash or a clash or a boom or a bang. It was the closest that cymbals can come to silence. It sounded like a chime in the wind. It lingered and floated and fell into the quiet time.

For a long while, no one spoke. No one moved. Everyone just sat and listened to the silence. Some may have dreamed.

When they finally started making their way home, Catina asked, "May I stay at your house tonight, Houndsley?"

"May I stay, too?" asked Bert.

"Of course," said Houndsley. Thinking about the refreshments they had forgotten to take to the concert, he added, "We may have to eat a lot of cookies."

Catina and Bert didn't mind. Eating cookies would be a perfect way to share the quiet time together.

Houndsley and Catina

Plink and Plunk

for Nathan and Kendra Lee

J. H.

Contents

Chapter One: Plink. 137

Chapter Two: Crash! 149

Chapter Three: Plunk 165

Chapter One
Plink

Houndsley loved to canoe.

Each spring he waited for the first warm day to take his canoe out on the lake.

His friend Bert usually went with him.

But this year Bert could not go.

"My aunt is in the hospital," said Bert. "I am going to visit her."

"You are a good nephew," Houndsley replied. "I will give you some vegetable soup to take with you."

"Does it have worms?" Bert asked. "Aunt Martha is fond of worms."

"It does not," said Houndsley. "But I could put some noodles in it."

“Noodles are almost as good as worms,”

Bert said. “Thank you, Houndsley.”

After Bert left, Houndsley wondered who else he might ask to go canoeing with him. He could invite his best friend, Catina. He liked doing everything with Catina. Everything, that is, but canoeing.

For some reason, whenever they went canoeing, Catina talked the entire time. She did not seem to understand that for Houndsley the joys of canoeing were the boat's silent glide over the water, the *plink* and *plunk* of the paddles, the calling of the birds as they swooped overhead, the rustle of the wind in the pines at the water's edge.

Perhaps, thought Houndsley, *this time will be different.*

It was not. From the moment Catina set foot in the canoe, she talked. And talked. And talked.

Houndsley could not hear the birds or the *plink* and *plunk* of the paddles. All he could hear was Catina's voice. *I wish she would stop talking*, Houndsley thought.

Suddenly, the canoe was caught in the wake of a passing boat. Up and down it went in the wavy water.

"Oh!" Catina cried.

"Hold on!" cried Houndsley.

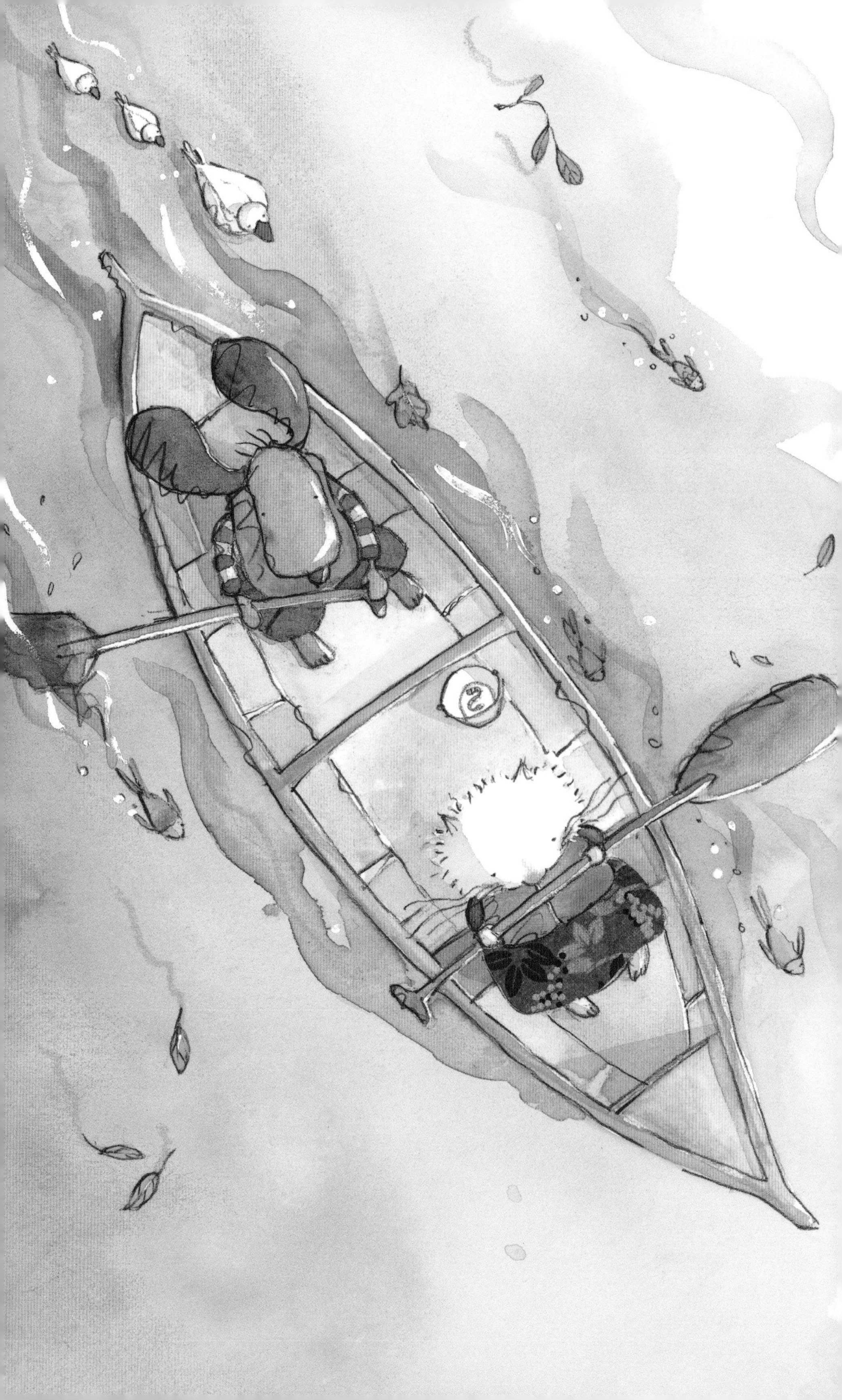

Catina gripped her paddle and clamped her eyes shut.

"Are you all right?" Houndsley called out to Catina when the water settled down.

Catina nodded her head but did not say a word.

At last Houndsley could enjoy the peace and quiet he wanted. But now that his wish had been granted, he began to worry. *What is wrong with Catina?* he thought. *Why has she stopped talking?*

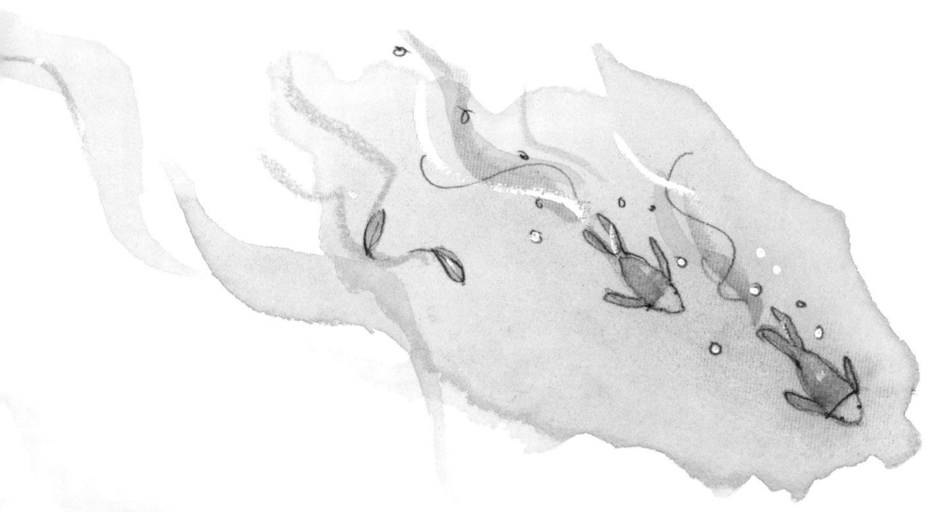

Chapter Two
Crash!

One morning Houndsley was working in his garden when he heard a *honk*. Mimi was delivering the mail.

"I have a package for you!" Mimi called out. "It's so big that I will need your help."

Just then, Catina came by on her bicycle.

"What is it?" Catina asked.

"I don't know," said Houndsley. "It's a surprise." He opened the envelope that was on the outside of the box and read the note inside:

Dear Cousin Houndsley,
I was doing my spring cleaning and found this.
I don't use it anymore. I seem to remember that you do not have one. Now you do!
Have fun!
Love,
Cousin Wagster

“A bicycle!” Catina cried out when the box had been opened.

Houndsley didn’t say anything. He thought of the bicycle he had just given away in his own spring cleaning. Cousin Wagster had forgotten that Houndsley owned a bicycle because Houndsley had never ridden it.

"Biking is one of my favorite things to do," Catina exclaimed. "We have never done it together, Houndsley. Why is that?"

Before Houndsley could answer, she went on, "Well, there is no time like the present. Let's go for a ride!"

Houndsley looked down at his feet. "Perhaps we could go next week," he said to Catina. "I have to plant my garden and . . . and . . ."

"You can plant your garden this afternoon," Catina said. "I will help you."

"It might rain," Houndsley said, his soft-as-a-rose-petal voice growing softer with each word.

"There is not a cloud in the sky," Catina replied. "Mimi, would you like to go with us?"

“I have more mail to deliver,” said Mimi. “But thank you for asking.”

“I’ll go with you,” said a new voice. No one had seen Bert arrive from his house

next door. "I'll get my bicycle—well, it is really a tricycle—and be right back!"

Oh, dear, thought Houndsley. *I do not want to go for a ride. But how do I say no?*

A few minutes later, the three friends set off. Catina led the way, followed by Bert, and slowly, slowly by Houndsley.

Houndsley wibbled. Houndsley wobbled.

Houndsley's feet flew up in the air.

Crash!

Houndsley landed in a cluster of azalea bushes. He held on to his helmet while his upside-down bicycle wheels went spinning.

“Are you all right?” Catina cried.

Houndsley nodded.

“Houndsley,” said Bert, “do you not know how to ride a bicycle?”

Feeling his face grow hot, Houndsley said in almost a whisper, “How did you guess?”

Bert began to laugh. Catina laughed, too. And soon Houndsley was laughing so hard, tears came to his eyes.

“Let’s trade,” said Bert when they were done laughing. “You can begin with three wheels, and before you know it, you will be ready for two!”

Chapter Three
Plunk

Houndsley packed a picnic lunch, and the three friends went for a long bicycle ride. He felt much safer on Bert's tricycle, and it wasn't long before he was willing to try his own two-wheeler again.

"You're doing it!" Bert cried as Houndsley pedaled down a country lane.

Houndsley wibbled. And Houndsley wobbled. But Houndsley stayed out of the azalea bushes and even stopped the bike by himself without falling over.

"Hooray for Houndsley!" Catina and Bert shouted.

As they spread their lunch on the blanket Houndsley had packed, Catina said, "There is something I must tell you, Houndsley. Do you remember how I talked so much when we went for our canoe ride?"

Houndsley did not want to hurt his friend's feelings, so he said, "Hmm, I'm not sure I do. But I remember how quiet you got after we almost tipped over."

"Yes," said Catina. "I got quiet because I was scared. And I was talking for the same reason. I talk a lot when I'm nervous."

"But what makes you nervous about canoeing?" Houndsley asked.

"I . . . I don't like water," Catina admitted. "I do not know how to swim."

"But you have gone canoeing with me many times," said Houndsley. "And have you been nervous every time?"

Catina nodded.

Bert passed her a pickle.

"That does not sound like fun," said Houndsley. "I am sorry you didn't tell me."

"I didn't want you to feel bad. You are my friend, and I wanted to do what you wanted to do."

Houndsley understood. “That is why I agreed to go biking, even though I was nervous.”

“But then we taught you how to ride,” said Bert. “So now you don’t have to be nervous anymore.”

“And I will teach you how to swim,” Houndsley told Catina. “We will go to the lake tomorrow. Can you come with us, Bert?”

“Yes,” said Bert. “My aunt is out of the hospital. I think it was your vegetable soup that made her better. She said those were the best worms she ever had. I did not tell her they were noodles.”

The next day, Houndsley, Catina, and Bert went to the lake.

"You are very good at the dog paddle," Houndsley told Catina.

"Thank you," said Catina.

Soon the three friends took the canoe out on the water. Their paddles *plink*ed and *plunk*ed. The birds called as they swooped overhead. The wind rustled in the pines at the water's edge.

No one said a word. Not even Catina.

First edition in this format 2018

Houndsley and Catina
Library of Congress Catalog Card Number 2005050187
ISBN 978-0-7636-2404-0 (hardcover)
ISBN 978-0-7636-6638-5 (paperback)

Houndsley and Catina and the Birthday Surprise
Library of Congress Catalog Card Number 2006042580
ISBN 978-0-7636-2405-7 (hardcover)
ISBN 978-0-7636-6639-2 (paperback)

Houndsley and Catina and the Quiet Time
Library of Congress Catalog Card Number 2007940973
ISBN 978-0-7636-3384-4 (hardcover)
ISBN 978-0-7636-6863-1 (paperback)

Houndsley and Catina Plink and Plunk
Library of Congress Catalog Card Number 2007032002
ISBN 978-0-7636-3385-1 (hardcover)
ISBN 978-0-7636-6640-8 (paperback)

ISBN 978-1-5362-0326-4 (paperback collection)

18 19 20 21 22 23 LEO 10 9 8 7 6 5 4 3 2 1

Printed in Heshan, Guangdong, China

This book was typeset in Galliard and Tree-Boxelder.
The illustrations were done in watercolor, pencil, and collage.

Candlewick Press
99 Dover Street
Somerville, Massachusetts 02144

visit us at www.candlewick.com